Tiana
the Toy Fairy
The Land of Sweets

Join the **Rainbow Magic Reading Challenge!**

Read the story and collect your fairy points to climb the

To Tamsyn and Jack

Special thanks to
Rachel Elliot

ORCHARD BOOKS

First published in Great Britain in 2017 by The Watts Publishing Group

1 3 5 7 9 10 8 6 4 2

© 2017 Rainbow Magic Limited.
© 2017 HIT Entertainment Limited.
Illustrations © Orchard Books 2017

HIT entertainment

Brands and all associated logos and copyright owned by Toys AndMe
are used herein under licence. © Toys AndMe 2017

The moral rights of the author and illustrator have been asserted.
All characters and events in this publication, other than those clearly in the public domain,
are fictitious and any resemblance to real persons, living or dead, is purely coincidental.

All rights reserved.
No part of this publication may be reproduced, stored in a retrieval system, or transmitted, in any
form or by any means, without the prior permission in writing of the publisher, nor be otherwise
circulated in any form of binding or cover other than that in which it is published and without a
similar condition including this condition being imposed on the subsequent purchaser.

A CIP catalogue record for this book is available from the British Library.

ISBN 978 1 40835 084 3

Printed and bound in Great Britain by CPI Group (UK) Ltd, Croydon, CR0 4YY

MIX
Paper from
responsible sources
FSC® C104740

The paper and board used in this book are made from wood from responsible sources

Orchard Books
An imprint of Hachette Children's Group
Part of The Watts Publishing Group Limited
Carmelite House, 50 Victoria Embankment, London EC4Y 0DZ

An Hachette UK Company
www.hachette.co.uk
www.hachettechildrens.co.uk

Tiana
the Toy Fairy
The Land of Sweets

by Daisy Meadows

ORCHARD

www.rainbowmagic.co.uk

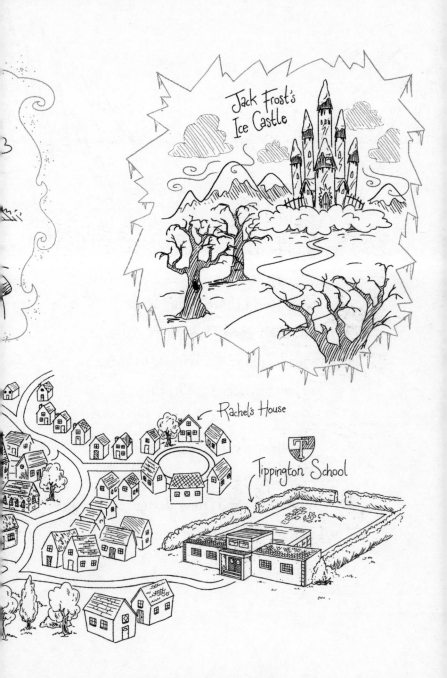

Jack Frost's Spell

I can't stand those flying fools
With all their goody-two-shoes rules.
They've made a land for friends to share,
Without inviting me in there.

Goblins, steal Tiana's key,
And bring her magic straight to me.
I want that candyfloss design.
The Land of Sweets must be all mine!

Contents

Disco Drama

Rachel Walker and her best friend Kirsty Tate were spinning around, holding each other's hands.

"Faster," Rachel cried. "Faster!"

"This is the best school disco I've ever been to," Kirsty shouted over the music.

"I'm so glad you could come," Rachel

shouted back. "It's twice as much fun with you here!"

All the other children around them were spinning too, and the DJ lowered the music for a moment.

"Great spinning!" he bellowed. "Now I want to see you all jumping, twirling, jigging and bopping."

He pushed up the volume again and soon the disco floor was packed with dancers, all twisting, wiggling and

swaying happily. Then Kirsty saw one of Rachel's teachers whisper something in the DJ's ear. He lowered the music.

"A little bird tells me that there's a bag of sweets for each person," he said. "It's time to go and collect your sweets, one class at a time. We'll start with Bluebird class."

Rachel's teacher went to stand behind a long table, which was filled with white paper bags. Rachel and Kirsty carried on

dancing, listening out for Rachel's class to be called. Then they noticed that the dance floor was emptying fast.

"Surely not everyone here is in Bluebird class?" asked Kirsty in surprise.

There was already a huge crowd of people around the sweets table, pushing and shoving to try to get to the front. Rachel and Kirsty stopped dancing and stared.

"Why are they pushing in?" Rachel asked. "There are enough sweets for everyone."

"Some of them are trying to take more than one bag," said Kirsty.

They watched some of the children snatch bags from others. A few of the smallest children started to cry, but the teachers weren't comforting them. They

were too busy shoving sweets into their own pockets!

"What's happening?" asked Rachel.

The dance floor was empty except for Rachel and Kirsty. Even the DJ had left his stand to get some sweets.

"Why is everyone being so mean?" asked Kirsty.

"I don't understand it," said Rachel. "Look – now the disco lights are going wrong too."

Most of the lights were still flashing red, green and blue, but one had a steady, golden glow.

"Rachel, look," said Kirsty in sudden excitement.

Rachel and Kirsty were good friends with the fairies, and they could always tell when there was magic in the air.

They got closer and saw Tiana the Toy Fairy sitting inside the light.

"Hello, Rachel and Kirsty," she said, waving to them. "I'm very glad to see you both."

The girls glanced around to check if anyone was looking, but everyone was busy trying to get as many sweets as they could.

"Let's duck down behind the DJ's stand," said Rachel. "Meet us there, Tiana."

The little fairy nodded, and the girls crouched down behind the stand. Tiana fluttered around to join them. She perched on Kirsty's knee, her wavy dark  hair bouncing around her shoulders. She was wearing a frilly white T-shirt and a pair of jeans, with a starry cardigan and orange sneakers.

"I bet you can guess why I'm here," she burst out.

"Is Jack Frost causing trouble again?" Rachel asked.

"Yes, big trouble," said Tiana. "It's going to affect the human world as well as Fairyland, so I have to stop him. Will you come to Fairyland with me so that I can explain?"

"Of course we will," said the girls. Tiana flashed them her beaming smile and raised her

wand. A fountain of magical fairy dust burst from the tip, and the girls instantly shrank to fairy size. They glimpsed a shower of tiny toys raining down around them. Then the toys turned into sweets of every size and colour, before becoming a

blur of reds, greens and yellows, whirling faster and faster. Fairy wings unfurled on their backs, and they felt Tiana's hands grasp theirs.

"Hold on tight," she called out.

The swirl of colours slowed down, and then shaped themselves into a little orchard of candy-laden trees.

"I know where we are," said Kirsty at once. "This is the Fairyland Sweet Factory."

The Land of Sweets

Several fairies came towards them
through the orchard, and the girls
recognised Honey the Sweet Fairy, Lizzie
the Sweet Treats Fairy and all seven of
the Sweet Fairies. Rachel and Kirsty
rushed forward to hug them all.

"We're so glad to see you again," said Coco the Cupcake Fairy. "We just wish it could have been for a happier reason."

"Last time we saw each other, you helped me get my magical marble back," said Tiana. "Since then, sweets everywhere have tasted delicious again. Everything has been great – until today. You see, Jack Frost has taken the key to the Land of Sweets."

"Fairies love to create surprises for each other," said Lottie the Lollipop Fairy, "and the Land of Sweets is our brand-new treat for all the fairies."

"It's a floating candyfloss cloud," Tiana went on. "It's meant to drift on the breeze above Fairyland, controlled by a magical candy key that I wear around my neck on a red ribbon."

"It sounds magical," said Kirsty. "But what happens there?"

"It's a place for fairies to enjoy the most delicious treats that the Sweet Factory makes," said

Esme the Ice Cream Fairy, "as well as Tiana's latest toy inventions."

"The idea is that every day, I will surprise one fairy by giving her the key to the Land of Sweets," said Tiana. "For that day, the Land of Sweets is hers to share with as many of her friends as she can. They can play with my latest toys and share delicious treats there, while the Land of Sweets floats across the sky. No one knows where it will go – not even us. It's a sort of magical mystery tour of Fairyland."

"That sounds amazing," said Rachel. "But if you don't know where the Land of Sweets will go, how can you bring it back each day?"

"I will place a new enchantment on the key each day," said Tiana. "The key will bring the Land of Spells to the fairy's home at sunset, and I will collect it ready for the next fairy."

"Just imagine," said Clara the Chocolate Fairy, clasping her hands together. "The candyfloss cloud shapes

itself into whatever you need, so there will always be enough seats around the Sharing Table."

"The Sharing Table?" Kirsty repeated.

"It's at the centre of the cloud, and it's always filled with toys and delicious treats," Madeleine the Cookie Fairy explained. "It's where friends can gather and enjoy their favourite sweets together."

"We were ready to give the first fairy an awesome surprise tomorrow," said Tiana. "But somehow, Jack Frost heard about the Land of Sweets and this morning he sent his goblins to raid my toy workshop."

"And they stole the candy key?" asked Rachel.

Tiana nodded. "They took it to Jack Frost," she said. "He used it to call the Land of Sweets to him."

"So now Jack Frost is in control of the Land of Sweets?" said Kirsty.

"It's not just that," said Tiana. "The key does a lot more than control the Land of Sweets. Its magic also makes sure that friends everywhere share and enjoy sweets together."

"Is that why everyone was being

so horrible at the disco?" Rachel asked.

Tiana nodded. "Without the key, no
one in Fairyland or the human world
will want to share their sweets," she said.
"We're all hoping that you can help us.
It's a disaster."

"Of course we'll help," said Kirsty.
"With all of us working together, I know
we can stop Jack Frost."

"I will come with you," said Tiana.
"The other fairies will stay here, using
their magic to try to protect the human
world while this is happening."

"Yes," said Lizzie the Sweet Treats
Fairy. "If people don't want to share
their sweets, friends and families will
start to fall out."

Rachel took Tiana's hand and
squeezed it.

"The three
of us defeated
Jack Frost last
time," she
said. "We
will do it
again."

"We
should start
by going
to the Ice
Castle," said Kirsty.

The other fairies gathered around them.

"We know you can do it," said Honey,
smiling at them. "Goodbye, and good
luck."

Floating Jack Frost

Tiana, Rachel and Kirsty waved, and then zoomed into the air and sped towards the freezing corner of Fairyland where Jack Frost lived.

"It's green!" Tiana exclaimed, when they saw the castle.

It had turned the colour of goblin skin. Statues of goblins topped the turrets, and there were goblins dancing along the battlements, swinging on the entrance doors and dangling out of windows by their ankles.

"Look at the courtyard," said Kirsty.

Crumpled cupcake cases littered the floor and there was a pond of green slime in the centre. Several goblins were ducking others into the slime amid squawks of laughter.

"What are they doing?" Rachel asked in astonishment.

"Causing chaos," said Tiana, folding her arms and shaking her head. "It's what they do best."

"There's no way they would be doing this if Jack Frost were here," said Kirsty.

They zoomed down and landed in front of a capering goblin. He stuck out his tongue and waggled his fingers at them, his thumbs in his ears.

"Excuse me, where is Jack Frost?" Rachel said.

"You don't belong here, pesky fairies," said the goblin. "Clear off. This is our castle now."

"Jack Frost won't like that," said Tiana, raising her eyebrows.

"He isn't coming back," said the goblin,

puffing out his chest. "Now we run the castle. He's stuck on that ugly pink cloud without his wand. Ha ha! He was in such a rush to explore it, he couldn't be bothered to go and fetch his wand from the Throne Room. How he yelled when it started floating away. Hee hee!"

"If Jack Frost is stuck on the Land of Sweets without his wand, he can't control it," Tiana said. "It is designed to float away as soon as the candy key is brought on to it. He won't be able to use the power of the key, or to choose where to go."

"He's never coming back," whooped another goblin, turning cartwheels around them. "Now we're having all the fun!"

"Oh my goodness, look over there,"

said Rachel.

Another goblin was holding Jack Frost's wand and aiming it at the castle wall. A bolt of lightning hit the wall with a bang and made a hole. Looking around, the fairies saw other holes in the walls.

"Hee hee!" the goblin cackled.

"If Jack Frost doesn't come back soon, he won't have a castle to come back to," said Tiana.

"Can't you call the Land of Sweets back?" Rachel asked.

Tiana shook her head as three goblins leapfrogged around them.

"Usually the magic of the key makes sure that the Land of Sweets comes back at sunset each day," she said. "But because Jack Frost stole it, I hadn't enchanted it to return to any particular place at the end of the day. And my magic isn't strong enough to make the key come back to me."

"So the Land of Sweets will float wherever the wind takes it?" said Rachel.

"Yes, and it will never land," Tiana added.

"Jack Frost can't have understood how it worked, or he would never have stepped on to it without his wand," said Kirsty.

"I've got an idea," said Rachel suddenly. "I know you can't bring the key to us, but is your magic strong enough to make it tell us where it is?"

"A finding spell?" said Tiana. "That could work."

She raised her wand and pointed it upwards, straight at the gloomy snow clouds blanketing the sky.

"Land of Sweets, you hold the key.
Let it send a sign to me.
Shine a light to guide our way
So we can bring you home today."

A fountain of golden fairy dust burst from the wand and hit the cloud above them. The cloud sparkled and turned golden, then changed into the shape of a key. It moved away from the Ice Castle and the fairies followed it, flying over Goblin Grotto and away from the snow-tipped trees. The key only stopped when it was hovering over the glittering turquoise sea. Then it broke up into smaller clouds, which drifted away.

"The Land of Sweets has journeyed out over the ocean," said Tiana. "We must go to sea!"

The Candyfloss Cloud

Side by side, Rachel and Kirsty followed the Toy Fairy out over Party Rock, remembering the adventures they had shared there with Shannon the Ocean Fairy. Soon the shore was far behind them. They saw mermaids playing in the waves and swooped down.

"Have you seen a pink candyfloss cloud?" Kirsty called out.

The mermaids waved to them, but shook their heads. Further out to sea, the fairies spotted a pod of dolphins, but they hadn't seen the Land of Sweets either.

The wind whistled past the fairies' ears as they flew, and tiny specks of salt sprayed their skin. Now and then, they saw fish and mermaids under the rippling water. At last, Tiana stopped and turned to face Rachel and Kirsty.

"We must be going in the wrong direction," she said. "There's no sign of the Land of Sweets."

Just then, a merry voice called to them from below. A familiar head broke through the water.

"It's Bubbles the seahorse," said Rachel, smiling. "It's wonderful to see you again."

They swooped down and fluttered around Bubbles as he bobbed in the water. They had met him when they were helping Rihanna the Seahorse Fairy. Now he looked older and  wiser, but he still had the same friendly expression.

"I know what you are looking for," he called to them. "The candyfloss cloud is floating over Paradise Island, far out in the middle of the ocean. Keep going — you will find it."

"Thank you, Bubbles," said Kirsty. "Goodbye!"

The three fairies had a long journey. The wind and spray made it hard to flutter their delicate wings. They dropped lower and lower.

"I can't fly much longer," said Rachel, panting.

"You won't have to," said Tiana, reaching for her hand. "Look."

There was an island up ahead, and hovering above it was a fluffy candyfloss

cloud. With one last burst of energy,
the three fairies fluttered upwards and
dropped on to the soft candyfloss.

"I've never flown such a long way," said
Kirsty.

"I wish you were here for a happier
reason," said Tiana. "But welcome to the
Land of Sweets."

She crawled over to a little patch of
bell-shaped blue flowers. Then she picked
three of the flowers and shared them out.

"Use these like cups," she said. "They
have honey nectar inside."

Rachel and Kirsty sat up and sipped
their cups. They tasted a sweet, refreshing
drink.

"It's like liquid gold," said Kirsty, licking
her lips.

"I feel better already," Rachel added.

"It's delicious."

"You can even eat the cups," Tiana added. "They're made of candy."

"This place is amazing," said Kirsty. "All my tiredness has melted away."

"I love it here," said Tiana, rising into the air and twirling around. "If you feel ready, let's head towards the Sharing Table at the centre."

As Tiana led the way past trees and plants, a delicious smell drifted on the breeze. It was like being in a gigantic sweet shop.

Rachel and Kirsty were delighted to see lollipops growing out of the ground like tall flowers.

"The soil is made from crumbled chocolate cookies," said Tiana. "That was Madeleine's idea."

Pear drops hung from little plants, and low sugared shrubs were dotted

with heart-shaped sweets wrapped in crackly coloured paper.

"Try one," said Tiana. "They're my favourites."

The sweets

were delicious, and Tiana smiled as the
girls enjoyed them.

"The tree trunks are made of
chocolate," she went on as they fluttered
between the trees. "And the branches are
sticks of rock with 'Fairyland' written
through them. Oh, look! These are the
yummiest!"

Tiana flew up to the branches
and picked a handful of
jelly babies, rocked
in pastel-coloured
rice-paper cradles.
The green sugared
leaves rustled
in the breeze,
and bunches of
rainbow-coloured
barley sugar twists dangled from the

trees like cherries, as well as puffy
marshmallows, lemon sherbets, orange
creams and peppermint fondants. And
whenever the fairies brushed against the
trees, they sent rice-paper flying saucers
swirling through the air like sycamore
seeds.

Rachel and Kirsty were so enchanted
by the amazing things they saw that they

almost forgot why they were there. They were quite surprised when they heard a rowdy, raucous noise coming from up ahead.

"We're getting close to the centre," Tiana whispered. "That sounds like goblins!"

Caged In!

The three fairies fluttered forwards and saw a clearing among the sweet trees and plants. In the middle, goblins were sitting on candyfloss chairs around a large table.

Platters of cakes and sweets had been trampled on, and goblin footprints criss-crossed the table. Some goblins were stuffing sweets into their mouths, their faces smeared with chocolate, icing sugar, jam and buttercream. Others were squabbling over toys. Drinks had spilled across the table and were dripping on to the sugared grass beneath.

"Oh, no!" said Tiana. "This is supposed to be a place to share sweets and play games with friends. It's not meant for litterbugs and toy breakers."

There was a bellow of rage and a thump of fists on the table. One enormous chair had its back to the fairies, and they saw a spiky head rise up from it.

"Be quiet, you ridiculous rowdy rabble!" yelled a familiar voice. "You're supposed to be working out how to turn this heap of fluff around and take me home!"

"It's Jack Frost," said Kirsty in alarm. The Ice Lord turned to glare at a goblin who was cartwheeling around the table, and Tiana gasped.

"My candy key is around his neck," she said. "We have to get it."

The striped key was

dangling from a bright-red ribbon.

"We will get it," said Rachel. "But we can't just fly out there in front of everyone."

"Couldn't we use the magic of the Land of Sweets?" said Rachel. "Clara said that the candyfloss would shape itself into whatever we need."

Tiana's eyes sparkled.

"That's an awesome idea," she said,
pressing her wand against a little mound
of candyfloss.

"Land of Sweets, we need your aid –
A tunnel through this candy glade.
To Jack Frost's chair please let us creep,
Where not a goblin eye can peep."

At once, the candyfloss opened up a
fairy-sized gap. Tiana hurried inside,
followed by Rachel and Kirsty. They
fluttered along a tunnel, lit by a faint
pink glow. Their wing tips brushed
against the fluffy walls. The tunnel was

not long, and the fairies came out just behind Jack Frost's chair. The Ice Lord was sitting in his vast chair again.

"It's lucky that Jack Frost gave himself the biggest, most important-looking chair of all," said Kirsty. "It hides us from all the goblins."

Just then, Jack Frost started yelling again.

"Will you rabble stop gobbling sweets for five minutes?" he demanded. "I'm sorry I ever brought you along. As long as we have to be stuck here, I don't want to listen to a crowd of munching, slurping goblins!"

"Goodness, he sounds grumpier than ever," Rachel whispered.

"Let's reach around the chair, one side each," Kirsty suggested. "Maybe together we can lift the ribbon from his neck before he notices."

They peeped around the chair and saw that all the goblins had their heads down, busily cramming more sweet treats into their mouths. Slowly, carefully, they stretched their hands towards the ribbon around Jack Frost's neck.

"Gotcha!"

Each girl felt one of Jack Frost's cold hands wrap around her wrist. They were pulled around to the front of the chair, and the Ice Lord glared at them, still holding them tight.

"I heard your silly little wings flapping," he snapped. "You'll be sorry for trespassing on my land."

"It isn't your land," said Rachel, trying to sound braver than she felt. "The Land of Sweets belongs to the fairies, and we are here to take it back."

Tiana zoomed around the chair to stand beside her friends.

"Give back the key you stole from me," she said.

Jack Frost leaned forward until his nose was almost touching Tiana's nose.

"You're my prisoners," he hissed. "You don't give me orders. I know how this place works!"

He let go of Rachel and Kirsty, and pointed a bony finger at the candyfloss under their feet.

"To deal with these unwelcome guests,
Make a cage for fairy pests.
Put them under lock and key,
And never ever set them free!"

At once, the candyfloss around the fairies rose up in bars, and they found themselves inside a huge birdcage. They *were* prisoners!

Return of the Candy Key

Kirsty folded her arms and glared at Jack Frost.

"You have trapped us before, and we have escaped before," she said. "We will escape again. But you cannot fly away

or make the Land of Sweets take you
back to the Ice Castle."
Jack Frost stuck his
fingers in his ears.
"Blah blah blah,"
he said rudely. "I'm
not listening."
"You will
have all the
sweets in the
world, but you are the
one who is really trapped,"
Kirsty went on. "And while you are stuck
here, the goblins are destroying your
castle."

Jack Frost took his fingers out of his
ears and sat up straight.

"What do you mean?" he growled.

"We saw them blasting holes in the

64

walls with your wand," said Tiana.

Jack Frost's beard quivered in fury.

"Tiana is the only person who can control the Land of Sweets," Rachel added. "You just have to give her the key."

"Never!" Jack Frost shouted.

"Don't you want to go home?" Tiana asked.

Jack Frost turned away and slumped sulkily in his chair.

"It's a shame you have to lose your castle," Rachel went on. "I wonder what it will be like to live on the Land of Sweets for ever – with the goblins."

Jack Frost glanced up at her in dismay, but he said nothing. The sound of goblins chomping on sweets filled the air.

"They are very noisy eaters, aren't they?" said Kirsty after a while.

Jack Frost thumped the table with his fist and stood up.

"You irritating little beetles!" he grumbled. "Fine, come out of the cage and have the silly key. Just take me home!"

The door of the cage opened and the fairies hurried out. Jack Frost took the ribbon from around his neck and held out the key. Tiana took it, and Jack Frost scowled.

"Next time I'll bring my wand, so I can get home again," he said. "Then the Land of Sweets will be mine."

He scowled and let go of the key. Tiana placed the ribbon around her neck.

"Now you will see how the Land of Sweets should look," she said.

With a wave of her wand, the Sharing Table was clean and tidy, the plates were full and the toys were mended. At the same time, the candyfloss cloud zoomed

away from Paradise Island. Soon, it
was hovering over the Ice Castle. Tiana
tapped her wand on
the cloud under
Jack Frost's feet,
and a trapdoor
opened.

"You're home," said
Tiana.

Jack Frost
peered down
through the
trapdoor
and let out
a bellow
of rage.

"You menaces!" he shouted. "You messy,
hare-brained chumps! You'll be sorry for
this! Where's my wand?"

He jumped down to the castle, closely
followed by the sticky, sweet-covered
goblins. Tiana closed the trapdoor and
smiled at Rachel and Kirsty.

"Jack Frost has a lot of tidying up to
do," she said. "I feel a bit sorry for him.
Maybe I'll even surprise him with the key
one day."

"That would be a lovely thing to do,"
said Rachel, hugging the little fairy.

"Thank you both for everything," said
Tiana. "Without you, the Land of Sweets
would still be drifting over the sea."

"We're so happy to have been able to
visit this amazing place," said Kirsty.

"It's time for me to send you back to
your disco now," said Tiana. "But maybe
you could come and spend a day on
the Land of Sweets with me and the

other fairies soon?"

"We'd love that," said Rachel.

Tiana gave her wand a little flick, and a puff of pink candyfloss lifted the girls into the air and spun them around, faster and faster, like a magical fairground ride. Then, in the blink of an eye, they found themselves back at the school disco. They were whirling around to their favourite Angels song, Key to My Heart.

The dance floor was full, and a few

children were queuing up politely at the sweets table. A teacher was smiling as she handed out bags of sweets.

"Everything's back to normal," said Rachel in a relieved voice. "Wow, that must be the yummiest adventure we've ever had."

"I'm excited about visiting the Land of Sweets again one day," said Kirsty.

"Me too," said Rachel, spinning her best friend faster and faster. "But right now I'm just happy to be here – sharing the sweets and the disco!"

The End

**Now it's time for Kirsty and
Rachel to help...**

Sianne the Butterfly Fairy

Read on for a sneak peek...

"Where are we going?" asked Kirsty Tate
for the tenth time that morning.

Mrs Tate glanced at her in the rearview
mirror, and her eyes twinkled.

Mr Tate turned around to look at his
daughter. "Haven't you guessed yet?" he
asked, smiling.

The car slowed down and turned on to
a narrow road. Kirsty bounced up and
down in her seat and gave a squeal of
excitement as she recognised the road.

"What is it?" asked her best friend,
Rachel Walker, who was sitting beside her.

"There's only one thing at the end of

this road," said Kirsty. "We're going to the Wetherbury Butterfly Centre, right, Mum? I've wanted to visit it ever since it opened last year."

"I thought that it would be the perfect time to visit, while Rachel is here for the weekend," said Mrs Tate. "You two always seem to have so much fun when you're together."

Rachel and Kirsty exchanged a secret smile. Mrs Tate knew about some of the fun times they had together, but she had no idea about the secret they shared. When they were together, magical adventures often seemed to follow them.

"Everyone says it's amazing there," Kirsty told Rachel. "There are lots of rare and exotic butterflies, and we can watch them coming out of chrysalises, and even go up in gliders to find out how it feels to fly."

Rachel couldn't help bouncing up and down as well. "Oh, I've always wanted to go gliding," she said. "This is going to be an incredible day."

Mrs Tate pulled into the car park and found a space. Soon they were all walking into the foyer of the Butterfly Centre. Pictures of butterflies decorated the walls, and Rachel and Kirsty looked at the butterfly toys, books and pens on sale while Mr and Mrs Tate paid.

A young man was standing in front of some double doors with a small group of people. He had brown hair and a cheerful, freckly face. He smiled when he saw them and beckoned them over. "You're just in time to join our tour group," he said. "I'm Fred, and I'll be your guide today."

Rachel and Kirsty said hello to the group. There were three teenage friends, a family with two small children, and an elderly couple called Mr and Mrs Bird, as well as two young women called Carly and Jane. Everyone seemed to be friendly and excited about their visit.

Read Sianne the Butterfly Fairy to find
out what adventures are in store for Kirsty and Rachel!

RAINBOW magic

Calling all parents, carers and teachers!
The Rainbow Magic fairies are here to help
your child enter the magical world of reading.
Whatever reading stage they are at, there's
a Rainbow Magic book for everyone!
Here is Lydia the Reading Fairy's guide to
supporting your child's journey at all levels.

① **Starting Out**
Our Rainbow Magic Beginner Readers are perfect for first-time readers who are just beginning to develop reading skills and confidence. Approved by teachers, they contain a full range of educational levelling, as well as lively full-colour illustrations.

② **Developing Readers**
Rainbow Magic Early Readers contain longer stories and wider vocabulary for building stamina and growing confidence. These are adaptations of our most popular Rainbow Magic stories, specially developed for younger readers in conjunction with an Early Years reading consultant, with full-colour illustrations.

③ **Going Solo**
The Rainbow Magic chapter books – a mixture of series and one-off specials – contain accessible writing to encourage your child to venture into reading independently. These highly collectible and much-loved magical stories inspire a love of reading to last a lifetime.

www.rainbowmagicbooks.co.uk

"Rainbow Magic got my daughter reading chapter books. Great sparkly covers, cute fairies and traditional stories full of magic that she found impossible to put down" – Mother of Edie (6 years)

"Florence LOVES the Rainbow Magic books. She really enjoys reading now" – Mother of Florence (6 years)

The Rainbow Magic Reading Challenge

Well done, fairy friend – you have completed the book!
This book was worth 5 points.

See how far you have climbed on the
Reading Rainbow opposite.

The more books you read, the more points you will get,
and the closer you will be to becoming a Fairy Princess!

Do you want your own Reading Rainbow?
1. Cut out the coin below
2. Go to the Rainbow Magic website
3. Download and print out your poster
4. Add your coin and climb up the Reading Rainbow!

There's all this and lots more at
www.rainbowmagicbooks.co.uk

You'll find activities, competitions, stories, a special
newsletter and complete profiles of all the
Rainbow Magic fairies. Find a fairy with your name!